Written by
Rosie Peet

Editorial Assistant Rosie Peet
Senior Editor Hannah Dolan
Designer Sandra Perry
Senior Designer Nathan Martin
Pre-Production Producer Marc Staples
Producer Louise Daly
Managing Editors Elizabeth Dowsett, Simon Hugo
Design Manager Ron Stobbart
Art Director Lisa Lanzarini
Publisher Julie Ferris
Publishing Director Simon Beecroft

Reading Consultant
Maureen Fernandes

First published in Great Britain in 2015 by Dorling Kindersley Limited
80 Strand, London, WC2R 0RL
A Penguin Random House Company

10 9 8 7 6 5 4 3 2 1
001–185648–Feb/15

A CIP catalogue record for this book
is available from the British Library.

ISBN: 978-0-24118-400-4

Colour reproduction by Altaimage, UK
Printed and bound in China by South China

www.dk.com
www.LEGO.com

A WORLD OF IDEAS:
SEE ALL THERE IS TO KNOW

Contents

Amazing Super Heroes

There are many Super Heroes in the universe. Some of the greatest heroes are Batman, Wonder Woman and Superman.

They each have amazing abilities that help them in their quest to keep the world safe. The villains of the world had better watch out!

4

Superman

Superman comes from planet Krypton. Now he lives on planet Earth in the city of Metropolis.

Superman hides his superpowers
by having another identity.
His other identity is a newspaper
reporter named Clark Kent.
No one knows that Superman
and Clark Kent are secretly
the same person.

Supergirl is another Super Hero
from planet Krypton.
She sometimes helps
Superman on
his missions.

Trouble in Metropolis

Lois Lane is a journalist for the *Daily Planet* newspaper. She writes news stories about Superman. Now she is about to become a news story herself!

General Zod, Faora and Tor-An are villains from Krypton. They have hatched an evil plot to capture Lois in their Black Zero Dropship.

Metropolis Rescue

Superman is on a rescue mission! General Zod is holding Lois captive inside his Black Zero Dropship. Can Superman save her?

Superman flies onto the Black Zero Dropship. General Zod puts on his armour and fights Superman. While Superman is battling Zod, Lois runs to the ship's escape pod. She flees to safety, while Superman defeats Zod.

Batman

Batman's mission is to protect Gotham City from crime. He fights villains with special gadgets and martial arts skills.

Just like Superman, Batman has another identity. Most people know him as the rich businessman Bruce Wayne. At night, Bruce puts on the Batsuit and fights criminals as Batman.

The Joker

The Joker is one tricky criminal.
He loves using wacky weapons
to cause mayhem on the
streets of Gotham City.

He is
planning
to attack
the city
on a crazy
steamroller.

The Joker has lots of henchmen that help him carry out his schemes. He makes them wear clown face paint to match his own face. They are too scared of the Joker to argue!

Battle for Gotham City

Whoosh! Here comes Batman
in his speedy Batwing.
He is rushing to defend
Gotham City from the Joker.

The Joker is attacking the city on his scary steamroller. It is flattening everything in its path! The Joker fires laughing-gas bombs, but the Batwing dodges them. Batman swoops down to stop the steamroller in its tracks.

Wonder Woman

Wonder Woman has some special tools that help her defeat villains. When villains are caught in her Lasso of Truth, they confess their crimes.

Wonder Woman also has an Invisible Jet. Her Invisible Jet can't be seen by her enemies, so she can use it to sneak up on them.

Heroes Unite

There is a terrifying new threat to the world's safety. A very strong and clever crook is planning a fiendish raid on Gotham City.

These Super Heroes will need to work together as a team in order to put a stop to this villain's monkey business...

Gorilla Grodd

Gorilla Grodd is an evil gorilla. He is very intelligent, and is always thinking about his next wicked plot. He has even invented a special mind-control device that he wears on his head.

His latest plan is to attack Gotham City and steal the city's bananas. Gorilla Grodd loves bananas and will stop at nothing to get his hairy hands on them.

Banana Battle

Gorilla Grodd is feeling hungry! He spots a banana delivery truck and decides to steal bananas from it. Greedy Grodd lifts the truck into the air and shakes it, sending the bananas flying. The poor driver is terrified!

Here comes Batman in his robotic Bat-Mech! He stomps towards Grodd. Uh-oh! Watch out for that banana, Batman! The Bat-Mech slips and falls with a crash. Batman needs help!

Super Heroes' Victory

Wonder Woman swoops in on her Invisible Jet. Gorilla Grodd can't see her! She takes aim and fires the jet's missiles at Grodd, taking him by surprise.

Next, Superman arrives and uses
his super-strength to deliver a
knockout blow to Gorilla Grodd.
Grodd is finally defeated!
The Super Heroes worked
as a team to save the day.
Well done, Super Heroes!

Quiz

1. Where does Superman live?

2. Which Super Hero uses special gadgets?

3. Which villain has a steamroller?

4. What does Gorilla Grodd like to eat?

5. What does Wonder Woman use to sneak past her enemies?

6. Where does General Zod hold Lois Lane captive?

7. Which Super Hero has a Lasso of Truth?

8. What is the name of Batman's other identity?

Answers on page 31.

Glossary

captive
unable to escape

confess
to tell the truth, or
own up to something

fiendish
wicked and mean

gadgets
useful devices

invisible
can't be seen

journalist
someone who writes
for a newspaper

martial arts
sports that teach
fighting skills
or self-defence

mayhem
a crazy, out of
control situation

unite
join together

victory
a big win

Index

Answers to the quiz on pages 28 and 29:
1. Metropolis 2. Batman 3. The Joker 4. Bananas 5. Her Invisible Jet
6. The Black Zero Dropship 7. Wonder Woman 8. Bruce Wayne

Have you read these other great books from DK?

The LEGO® Movie Awesome Adventures
Meet Emmet and join him on his
quest to save the universe!

LEGO® *Star Wars*™ **The Empire Strikes Back**
Can brave Luke Skywalker defeat
sinister Darth Vader?

Space Quest
Embark on a mission to explore the
solar system. First stop – Mars.

LEGO® Legends of Chima™ **Power Up!**
Discover the new tribes threatening Chima™
with their icy powers.

Hope for the Elephants
Join David on an amazing trip to meet
elephants in Asia and Africa.

Batman™'**s Missions**
Follow Batman as he fights to protect
Gotham City from crime.